# Walt Disney's
# Mickey Mous
# Hideaway Island

**gb GOLDEN PRESS**
Western Publishing Company, Inc.
Racine, Wisconsin

GOLDEN®, A GOLDEN BOOK® and GOLDEN PRESS® are trademarks of Western Publishing Company, Inc.

*Library of Congress Cataloging in Publication Data*

Walt Disney's Mickey Mouse, Hideaway Island. SUMMARY: Mickey Mouse retreats from one ambitious, noisy friend after another in his search for the ideal spot in which to relax in his new hammock. Then he realizes he has found more peace and quiet than he wants. [1. Friendship—Fiction. 2. Animals—Fiction] I.Title: Mickey Mouse, Hideaway Island. PZ7.M58193 [E] 80-13647
Library of Congress Catalog Card Number: 80-67143 ISBN 0-307-10829-5

"What a great day to try my new hammock!"
Mickey Mouse said to Pluto. "I'll hang it between those
trees, have some lemonade, and listen to my radio. Then
I'll take a nice, long nap."

Pluto wagged his tail. The sun was shining, and the
breeze was warm. *He* wanted a nice, long nap, too.

Mickey climbed into his hammock. He had just dozed off
when loud cheering from the yard next door woke him up.

"Oh, my!" Mickey said. "I can't take a nap with all
that noise."

Mickey peeked over the fence. There was Horace Horsecollar, watching his favorite television show, with the sound turned up as loud as it would go.

"Horace is having such a good time," Mickey told Pluto. "Let's take the hammock to Goofy's house. Maybe it's quieter over there."

But it was far from quiet at Goofy's house. Goofy was fixing his car, and he was making all sorts of pounding and rattling noises. Right away Mickey gave up the idea of resting.

"Can I help you, Goofy?" he asked.

Goofy was delighted to have a helper! First they fixed the
engine. Then they patched two flat tires.

"Thanks, Mick!" Goofy said. "Now that my car's finished,
let's fix the roof of my house. It leaks."

"Sorry, Goofy," Mickey said, "but I'm looking for a quiet
place where I can rest. I'll try Minnie's house."

Minnie Mouse wasn't fixing a car or a roof. She *was* painting her house!

Mickey sighed. "No nap here, either," he said. He put his hammock down, picked up a paintbrush, and began to paint.

"Wonderful!" cried Minnie. "And when we've finished the front door, we can start on the kitchen!"

"Let's paint the kitchen some other day," Mickey said. "I'm going to try out my new hammock at Clarabelle's."

But when Mickey and Pluto drove up in front of Clarabelle's house, they saw Clarabelle mowing her front yard.

"Oh, no!" Mickey said. "More noise. And more work!"

"Oh, Mickey," said Clarabelle, "I'm so glad to see you! You're just in time to help me move the rocks for my new rock garden."

Mickey sighed. It seemed that everybody needed his help today.

While Mickey was filling the wheelbarrow with rocks and wheeling them into the new garden, he was thinking of another place — a place that would surely be quiet and peaceful.

"Yoo-hoo!" Clarabelle called, startling Mickey out of his daydream. "It's time to start planting!"

"Some other day," Mickey said. "I just thought of somewhere I have to go."

Before long, Mickey and Pluto were sailing out of the harbor in Mickey's sailboat.

"Next stop, Hideaway Island!" Mickey said. "There aren't any old cars there. And there aren't any rock gardens or paintbrushes or noisy TV's."

Pluto sat on the deck and wagged his tail happily.

Hideaway Island was as quiet and peaceful as Mickey had hoped. He pulled his boat onto the beach, put up his hammock and climbed into it.

"This is terrific!" he said as he sipped lemonade and watched Pluto chase sea gulls along the beach.

In a little while, Mickey was sound asleep.

When Mickey woke up, the sun was low in the sky, the warm breeze had turned cool — and his boat was gone! The tide had come in and washed it out to sea!

"Oh, no!" Mickey said. "We can't get back home without our boat!"

"Woof?" said Pluto.

"Don't worry," Mickey said. "Somebody will find us — sooner or later. We'd better try to catch some fish for supper."

But catching fish wasn't easy without a fishing pole. Mickey had to chase the fish into shallow water and scoop them up onto the beach.

Mickey didn't have any matches, so he had to rub sticks together to start a fire. That wasn't easy, either.

Finally he got a small fire going. Sitting beside it, he broiled the fish and dried his clothes. Pluto howled — he didn't like the fish. He wanted his own dog food.

Soon the sun went down. The cool breeze became a cold wind. Mickey and Pluto huddled near the fire.

"Hideaway Island is peaceful and quiet, all right," Mickey said, "but it's lonely, too. I wonder if anyone's looking for us."

At last he and Pluto fell asleep.

Very early in the morning, Mickey awoke to the sound of familiar voices calling his name.

There were Goofy, Minnie, Horace Horsecollar, and Clarabelle Cow— in *his* sailboat!

Pluto barked loudly as Goofy steered the boat toward the island.

"When your boat drifted into the harbor, we figured out where you were," said Goofy.

"I guess we weren't very considerate yesterday when you wanted to try out your new hammock," said Clarabelle. "Next time, we'll do our own work and let you rest."

"I'll paint my kitchen myself," promised Minnie.

"And I'll plant my rock garden without any help," said Clarabelle.

"I'll fix my roof by myself," Goofy said.

"And I'll keep my TV set turned down," said Horace.

Mickey smiled. "Play your TV as loud as you like.
And ask me to help whenever you want to," he said.
"I've had enough peace and quiet on this island to last me
a long time."